For all you readers who welcomed Mercy into your hearts

K. D.

For Sylvie to read to Oliver

C. V.

First published in Great Britain 2019 by Walker Books Ltd
87 Vauxhall Walk, London SE11 5HJ

2 4 6 8 10 9 7 5 3 1

Text © 2019 Kate DiCamillo
Illustrations © 2019 Chris Van Dusen

The right of Kate DiCamillo and Chris Van Dusen to be identified as the author and illustrator respectively
of this work has been asserted by them in accordance with the Copyright, Designs and Patents Act 1988

This book has been typeset in Mrs Eaves

Printed in China

British Library Cataloguing in Publication Data:
a catalogue record for this book is available from the British Library

ISBN 978-1-4063-8868-8

www.walker.co.uk

A Piglet Named Mercy

Kate DiCamillo

illustrated by

Chris Van Dusen

WALKER BOOKS
AND SUBSIDIARIES
LONDON · BOSTON · SYDNEY · AUCKLAND

Mr Watson and Mrs Watson lived
in a house on Deckawoo Drive.

Deckawoo Drive was an ordinary street
in an ordinary town.

And Mr and Mrs Watson were ordinary people
who did ordinary things in ordinary ways.

One day, Mrs Watson said to Mr Watson,
"I wonder if we aren't just the tiniest bit
   too predictable."

"Predictable? Us?" said Mr Watson.
"Surely not."

"It's just that sometimes, I wish something
   different would happen," said Mrs Watson.

"Things are just fine as they are,"
   said Mr Watson.

But then something different *did* happen.

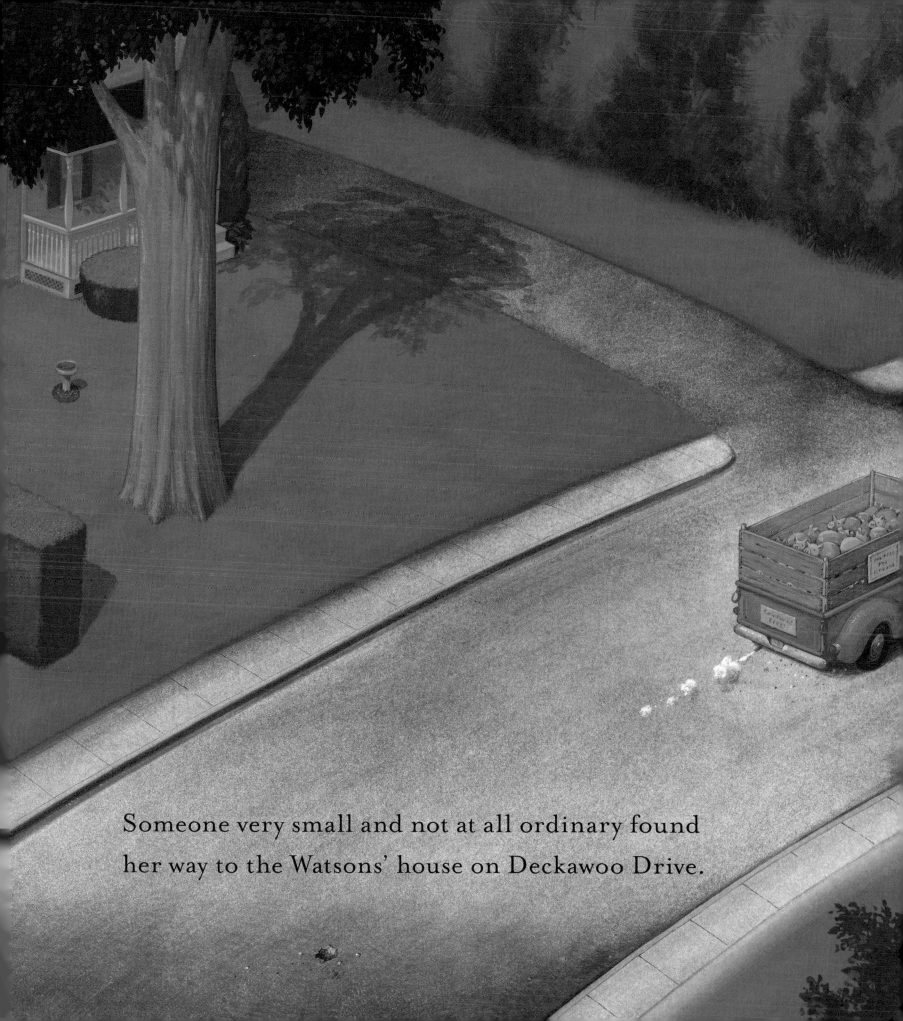

Someone very small and not at all ordinary found her way to the Watsons' house on Deckawoo Drive.

Mr Watson made the discovery when he opened the door for the morning paper. "Mrs Watson!" he called. "Come see!"

"Oh, the little dear," said Mrs Watson.

"Oink," said the piglet.

"I think she's hungry," said Mr Watson.

"Is that a pig?" said Eugenia Lincoln.
Eugenia Lincoln lived next door, and she
did not approve of surprises. Or pigs.

"It is!" said Mrs Watson. "Can you believe our luck?"

"Don't be ridiculous," said Eugenia Lincoln.
"A pig is not lucky at all."

"Do you think perhaps the piglet would like a bottle of warm milk?" said Baby Lincoln. Baby was Eugenia's younger sister, and she was fond of surprises. And piglets.

Mr Watson scratched his head. "A bottle of milk? I don't know... This is all so unpredictable."

"Leave it to me," said Baby Lincoln.

"Oink!" said the piglet again.

Mrs Watson picked up the piglet and took her inside. She wrapped her in a blanket. "Have you ever seen anyone so darling?" she said.

"Never," said Mr Watson.

"Here is the warm milk," said Baby Lincoln.

"I have it right here."

Eugenia said, "This is absurd."

The piglet did not think it was absurd at all. She drank the entire bottle.

And then she burped.

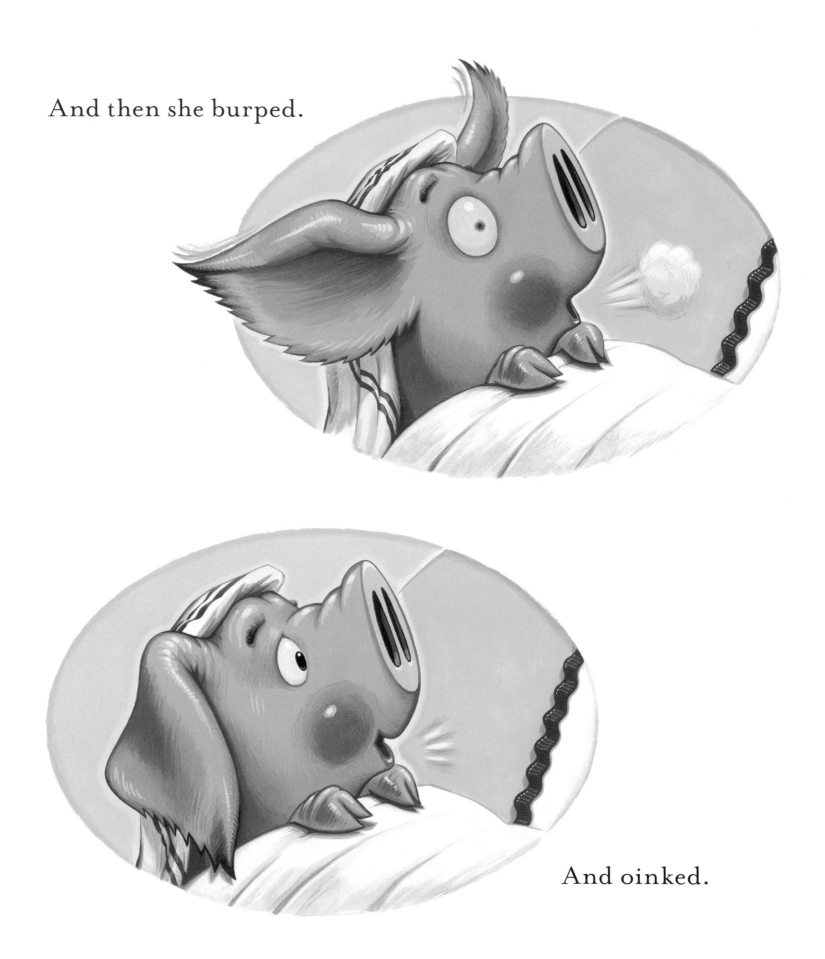

And oinked.

And went looking for more.

"Oh, my goodness," said Mr Watson.

"Watch out!" said Eugenia.

"She seems to like toast very much!"
said Baby.

"Oh, the darling, darling thing,"
said Mrs Watson.

"Mr Watson," said Mrs Watson, "perhaps you would like to hold her for a bit?"

"Certainly," said Mr Watson.

He took the piglet in his arms.

He rocked her.

He hummed.

"How extraordinary," said Mr Watson. "She is a porcine wonder."

"This piglet is a wish come true,"
  said Mrs Watson.

"What a mercy she is," said Baby.

"There you go," said Mr Watson.
"We will call her Mercy."

"She is not a mercy," said Eugenia.
"She is a pig."

"Oink, oink," said the piglet.

"You cannot name a pig Mercy!"
  shouted Eugenia.

But they did name her Mercy.

She was entirely unpredictable.

She was not at all ordinary.

And she was very, very loved.